The Princess, the Dragon, and the Baker

A Chanuka Fairy Tale

by Oren Litwin

art by Shir Dahan and Manthos Lappas

For Datya, my shining light

and

For Yosef, Devora, Ayla, Ezra, Talia, and Mira
for whom this story was first written.

Once, long ago in a faraway land, there was a wise princess who lived in a magical castle. The princess commanded a large fearsome dragon, who was strong enough to do all sorts of work that people needed.

If the people needed fish, the princess would tell her dragon to carry a giant net to the ocean and fish there. If the people needed a new road, the princess would have her dragon melt rocks with his fiery breath and pave the road with them. And the people were happy, because their princess took care of them.

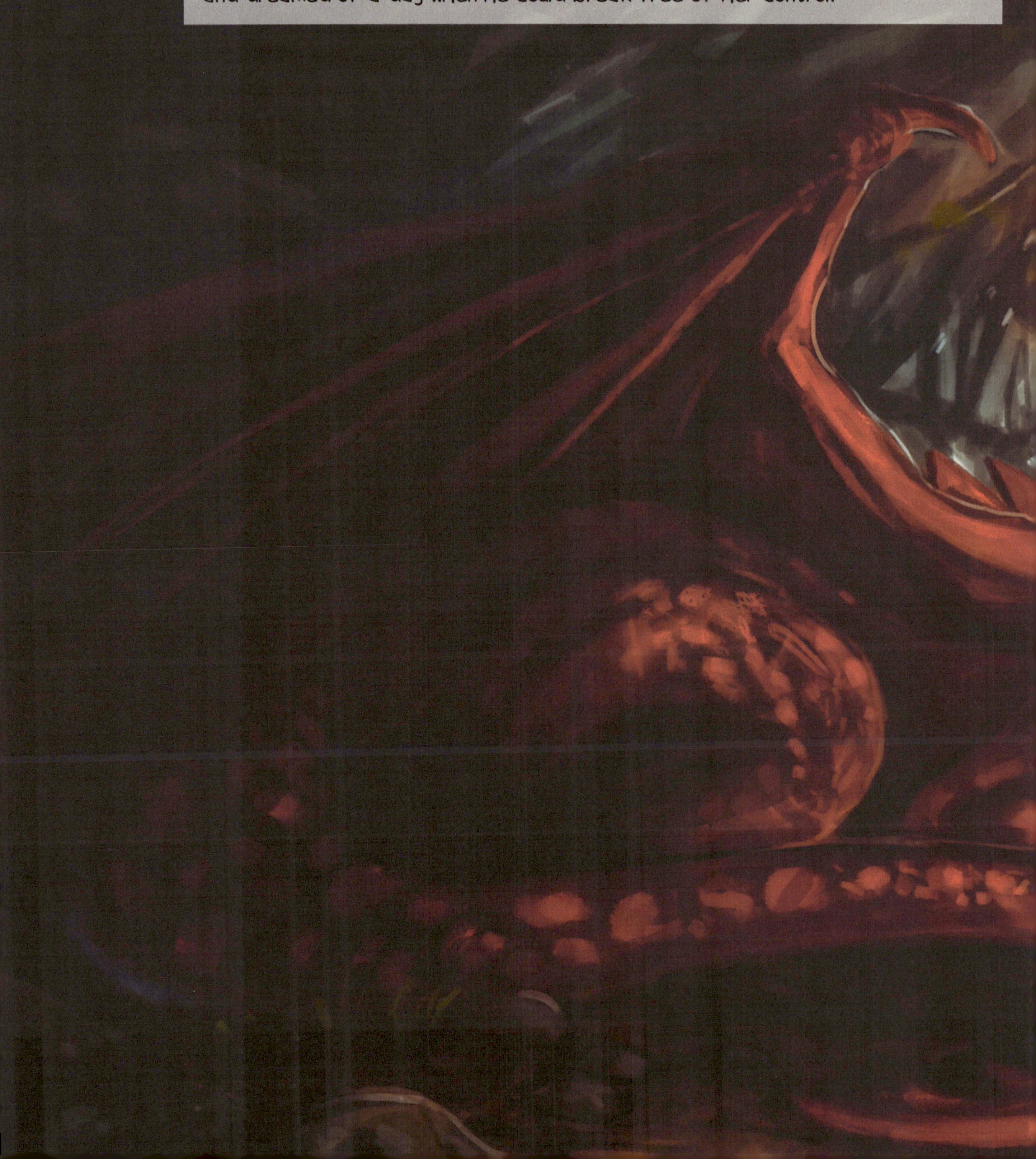

But the dragon was not happy. Not only was he doing all the work, but he was always hungry, because the princess wouldn't let him eat people. Imagine *you* were a dragon, and you were surrounded by happy people all the time, and you couldn't even eat one of them! So the dragon was very sore at the princess, and dreamed of a day when he could break free of her control.

At last, his chance came. The dragon used a powerful magic spell to send the princess into a deep sleep, and hid her away in her castle.

Then he flew out into the land, and ate dozens of sheep and cattle and even a few people. And the people were afraid, because their princess was gone and could no longer take care of them, and because the dragon's hunger was insatiable.

Many heroes ventured into the castle to save the princess, but none of them ever returned. The people lost hope that they would ever have their princess back.

But one man had not lost hope. Yet he was no great warrior, but a simple baker named Chanoch. And he had a plan.

One day, Chanoch came up the road to the castle, carrying a big heavy backpack, and cautiously crept inside.

He found the main hall covered by thick darkness; he couldn't even see the great throne where the princess sat, but he knew in his heart that she was there. Looking around the edges of the darkness, he saw four great oil lamps on the left side of the room, and four more on the right.

"If I light those," he said, "I'll be able to see the princess. Maybe then I'll know what to do."

But scarcely had he taken out his flint and tinder to light a torch, when the room rumbled as the dragon swooped down from the roof and landed on the floor with a thud.

"Oh no you don't!" he cried with a mighty roar. "I suffer a terrible hunger, and the princess would never let me satisfy it. So as long as the hunger remains, the princess will stay my prisoner!"

Oddly enough, this was just what Chanoch had expected. "Good sir
dragon," he said kindly, "of course I don't want you to go hungry. But have
you ever tried eating something other than people?"

The dragon paused and cocked his head. Normally, the heroes just went straight to the stabby stabby, and then he ate them. Chanoch's politeness was unusual. "Well," he said, "the princess fed me nothing but lettuce and tofu. It was all so bland. I needed something more. I needed to eat people!"

"I can understand that," Chanoch said. "But what if there were a food that was better than people?"

"Like what?" the dragon asked, curious.

For answer, Chanoch took out mixing bowls, a frying pan, and ingredients from his backpack: flour, water, sugar, eggs, and oil. He mixed dough, formed it into round balls, and put them into the pan with a little bit of oil. "Could you do the honors?" he said to the dragon.

The dragon was skeptical, but he breathed a short puff of fire onto the pan, frying the dough balls in the oil.

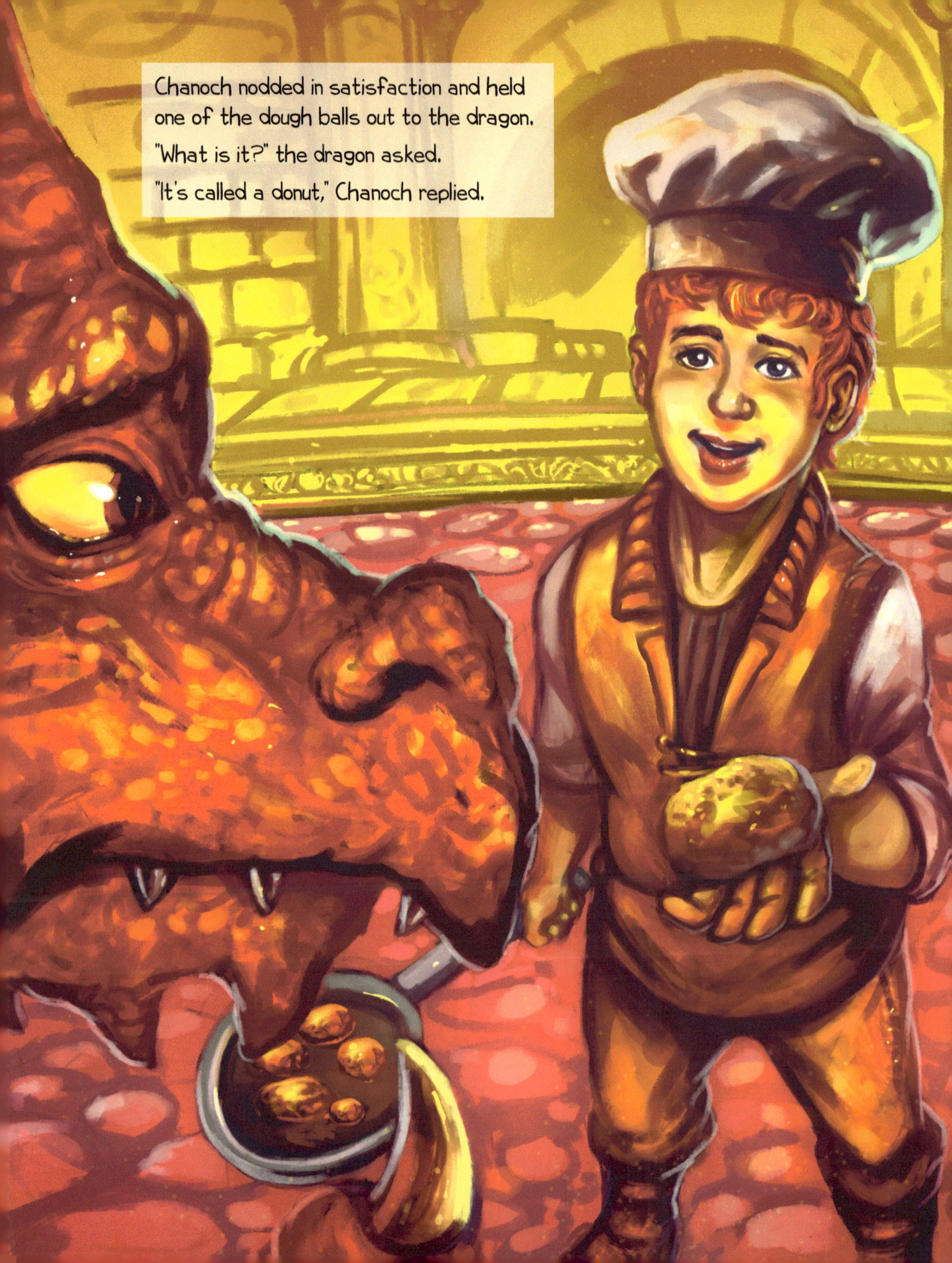
Chanoch nodded in satisfaction and held one of the dough balls out to the dragon.
"What is it?" the dragon asked.
"It's called a donut," Chanoch replied.

"Hmm," the dragon said. He snaked out his big head and snagged the donut with his long thin tongue, chomping on it with his giant pointy teeth. "Not bad," he said, surprised. "Nice and soft on the outside, and sweet and chewy on the inside. Kind of like people." But he hesitated. "It's still not as good as really eating people," he said. "There's something missing."

"Tell me," Chanoch said, "and I'll try to fix it."

"Well," the dragon said, concentrating on the taste, "when I eat people there's a gooeyness to it. The donut is too dry on the inside."

Chanoch smiled. "Easy enough." He took out a jar of strawberry jelly and a large syringe. Sticking the syringe into the center of a new donut, he squirted jelly inside, and sealed the hole with a little dough. He held it out to the dragon. "Try it now," he said.

The dragon ate the jelly donut, chewing slowly, little globs of jelly dripping onto his scaly lip until he licked them up. "Hey, this is good," he said. "Even better than before." But still he hesitated. "It's close, but it's still not quite the same."

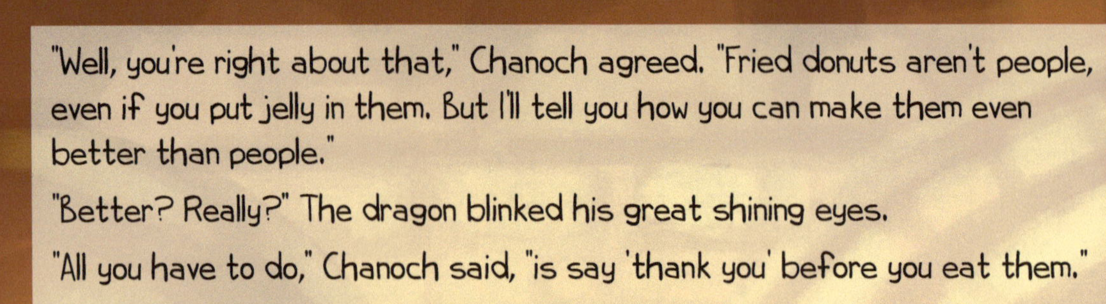

"Well, you're right about that," Chanoch agreed. "Fried donuts aren't people, even if you put jelly in them. But I'll tell you how you can make them even better than people."

"Better? Really?" The dragon blinked his great shining eyes.

"All you have to do," Chanoch said, "is say 'thank you' before you eat them."

The dragon laughed, smoke trailing from his mouth. "That's silly! How could saying 'thank you' make food taste better?"

Chanoch smiled. "Because saying thank you shows that you appreciate the food. Here, try it." He held out another jelly donut.

"I still think it's silly," the dragon said, "but all right." He snaked his head forward again, but before grabbing the donut, he said, "Thank you for this donut." Then he chewed and swallowed. As he did, the dragon's face glowed with delight. "Wow!" he said. "You were right! This is so much better than people."

"So does that mean you'll free the princess?" Chanoch said.
The dragon licked his lips, fidgeting. "Do you think the princess will let me eat these jelly donuts? Or will she make me go back to tofu?"
"If you say thank you for them, I'm sure the princess won't mind," Chanoch said. "And I promise you'll get all the jelly donuts you need."

"All right then," the dragon said. "I sealed the princess with a word of power. When you light the lamps, you'll be able to read it. Just speak it aloud, and she'll wake up."

So Chanoch lit the eight lamps, and their light drove away the darkness in the throne room. Just as he knew she would be, the princess was seated on her throne, fast asleep. Hovering in front of her was a glowing word, written in the air. Chanoch spoke it aloud, and it dissolved. The princess woke up.

"Sufgan!" she said. "You've been a very naughty dragon!"

"I know," the dragon said sheepishly. "But it's okay now, because Chanoch is going to give me jelly donuts to eat instead of people."

"That sounds better, Sufgan," the princess said. "Just as long as you're sorry, and you never do it again."

So everyone was happy. The princess was awake again and could take care of the people once more. This time Sufgan the dragon got to eat jelly donuts, so he didn't mind working. And he always said thank you to Chanoch.

The people were glad that their princess had been
returned to them, so much so that they made a holiday
in Chanoch's honor, which they called Chanuka. They even
forgave Sufgan the dragon, and called his jelly donuts
Sufganiot. Even today, we eat sufganiot on Chanuka to
commemorate when the princess and the dragon started
working together again.

So now, dear readers, have a happy Chanuka. And remember that when your own dragons get hungry, it's better to eat jelly donuts than to eat people. And don't forget to say thank you!

For Parents

On the simple level, Chanuka is about the military victory of the Maccabees over the Syrian Greek occupiers. But on a more profound level, Chanuka really addresses the relationship between the physical and spiritual, and how each should be a part of our lives. In this story, the princess represents the Godly side of us, disregarding physical pleasure while seeking to achieve spiritual heights. The dragon represents our animalistic side, chafing under restrictions and seeking to gratify itself with physical pleasures.

Initially the princess imposed herself totally on the dragon, neglecting his own needs and wants. That is the ascetic model of life, which Judaism generally frowns on. Then the dragon broke free of the princess, rejecting lofty goals and gorging itself physically. That is the hedonistic model of life, which Judaism also avoids.

The Jewish approach is symbolized by Chanoch. Rather than controlling the dragon by force, he gently taught the dragon how to redirect physical desires in a more elevated direction. Expressing gratitude, as we do with the blessings over food, is but the first step in our task of bringing the Divine into this world, making the physical into something spiritual rather than rejecting one for the sake of the other.

Ask your family: Can you think of one way that you can bring spiritual meaning into something physical?

About the Author

Oren Litwin lives with his family in northern Virginia, where he works in public policy. This is his second book, the first being *The Best Congress Money Can Buy: Stories of Political Possibility*. He blogs about his writing and how societies work at http://orenlitwin.com.

www.ingramcontent.com/pod-product-compliance
Lightning Source LLC
Chambersburg PA
CBHW041135100726
47911CB00003B/129